Classic
Stories

Two Wise Children

written by Robert Graves ● illustrated by Venitia Dean

The
Child's
World

Published by The Child's World®
1980 Lookout Drive • Mankato, MN 56003-1705
800-599-READ • www.childsworld.com

Acknowledgments
The Child's World®: Mary Berendes, Publishing Director
Red Line Editorial: Editorial direction
Emily Love: Design and production

ISBN 978-16232-36243
LCCN 2014931027
Printed in the United States of America
Mankato, MN
July, 2014
PA02213

4

A boy called Bill Brain, a minister's son, lived in New England near the sea. One Tuesday morning in summer he went for a walk through the fields, picking blueberries into a tin can. Half a mile from home he passed a big house which some newcomers to the town had just bought. They were Colonel and Mrs. Deeds and he had first met them on the Sunday before, outside his father's church. Colonel Deeds watched birds, and Mrs. Deeds drove fast cars. Avis, their only daughter, had fair pigtails, a sunburned face, white teeth, and a snub nose. Bill felt shy with girls, having no sisters. But something about Avis had struck him at once. It seemed as though he had known her for years and years, and as though they shared a big secret. And he guessed that she felt the same about him because her smile wasn't just a polite smile of welcome, but one that meant, "Oh, there you are at last!" Avis was eight, and Bill two years older!

The day before, when Bill had awakened from a bad dream, he remembered that Avis had come into it, and that he had dreamed the same thing two or three times since Christmas. He couldn't say exactly what had happened in the dream, except that he was being watched by a huge, jeering crowd while some big black animal tried to kill him, and that suddenly Avis flew down from a tree and said, "It's all right, Bill. The bandages are in father's medicine chest." He thought to himself, "What a crazy dream!" Yet it still seemed real to him in a way, and he couldn't laugh it off. He couldn't even bring himself to tell his mother and father about it at breakfast.

Well, now it was Tuesday morning. And as he passed the Deeds's big house with the blueberry can slung around his neck, he suddenly said to himself, "How could I have dreamed about Avis long before I met her? Or did I just dream that I had already dreamed the same thing two or three times before?" Bill could see nobody in the Deeds's garden, and he didn't like to shout "Avis, are you there?" So he went on towards Robson's farm, which lay hidden behind a wood. The best blueberry bushes grew on a small rocky hill nearby and he went up it, picking fast into the can, which was already half full. A few minutes later he reached the top and saw something very curious on the other side.

There stood Avis on the back of Robson's white horse, with one foot lifted like a dancer's, her arms spread out, and a hay rake balanced upright on her chin, while the horse galloped around the field!

"That girl must have worked in a circus," he thought. But in case she might not like being watched, he went back behind the hilltop, picked blueberries for another five minutes or so, and then came up again whistling loudly. Avis had got down from the white horse and now sat on a rock with her head bent over some work or other.

She heard Bill's whistle. "There you are at last," she said. "I expected you five minutes ago. Where have you been?"

But Bill was looking at a small square of white linen which she held crumpled in her hand. "Is that what you have been sewing?" he asked. "Let me look!"

"Oh, it's not worth anything," Avis said. "This is the first time I've done needlework. I borrowed mother's colored silks. It's taken me most of the morning."

"What else have you done?"

"Oh, eaten a few blueberries and tried riding Farmer Robson's horse."

"I suppose that was the first time you ever rode a horse?" Bill asked, to tease her.

But Avis said seriously, "Yes, the first time ever, but I got along quite well."

Bill took the crumpled square of linen from her hand, and found on it the most wonderful needlework he had ever seen. It was a silk picture of flowers and butterflies sewn in about thirty different colors with hundreds of tiny stitches. Only one flower and half a butterfly were not yet finished.

"Did you copy a pattern?" Bill asked.

"No," said Avis.

Bill looked her straight in the eyes. He said, "I saw you riding the horse. I hope you don't mind. And now there's this marvelous needlework. Explain, please. . . ."

"Oh, I didn't mind being watched by *you*," said Avis. "And there's nothing much to explain, really. I wanted to do a circus act, so I just did it, because I knew how. And I wanted to make this needlework picture in colored silks, so I just did it because I knew how."

"Oh, I *see*!" said Bill.

"What do you see?" asked Avis.

"I see what's happened to you. It's like what happened to me last spring in a field near our house. I was alone, and the dogwoods had just begun to flower, and hundreds of birds sang, and the world seemed changed and *right*."

"Yes," said Avis. "That's just how I felt when I first came to this field. Go on!"

Bill went on, "Suddenly I found that I knew everything. I had only to tilt my head a little and ask myself any question I pleased, and the answer came at once."

"What *sort* of things?"

"Well, I had often wondered who first built our house and when he built it. So I tilted my head and knew that a Scotch blacksmith called Sawney Todd and his son Robb had built it in 1656. And somehow I knew that if I dug down four or five inches under my left heel, I'd find an old gold brooch belonging to Ruth Todd, Sawney's wife. So I cut out a piece of turf with my knife and found the brooch. It had 'R.T. 1654' scratched on the back."

"Did that scare you? *I* got a scare at first by things going marvelously right like that. I'm used to them now."

"It did scare me a little. Then I went home and there was my Uncle Tim arguing with Father about some law business. They had a lot of papers spread on the table, written in very difficult English. Uncle Tim was being rather rude to my father, so I said, 'You're wrong, I'm afraid, Uncle Tim.' And I picked the papers up, read out one of the most difficult ones to him, and showed him just where he had made his mistake. They both looked at me in such surprise that I got all red and explained, 'You see, I know everything today.' Father frowned at me for boasting, but Uncle Tim laughed and asked, 'All right, Bill, if you know everything, what horse will win the big race on Saturday?' I tilted my head, and then told him, 'A big black horse called Gladiator will win. It's ridden by Sam Smile.'"

Avis interrupted. "I don't *know* everything, Bill; it's just that I can *do* everything. It's a bit different. Do you still know everything?"

Bill sighed. "No, I don't, Avis. That's what I want to warn you about, if you don't mind. Take care not to let anyone but me into your new secret. I made a terrible mistake over mine."

"What sort of a mistake?" Avis asked.

"It had to do with money. My Uncle Tim went off to town and bet a hundred dollars that Gladiator would win the race, and it did. He made a thousand dollars from the bet, and gave me a ten-dollar bill for myself, and told all his friends about my knowing everything. One of them asked me what horse would win the next big race. I tried to tell him, but somehow no answer came. Then I hoped that I'd know if I saw a list of all the horses that were going to run. The man showed me a list, but still I couldn't tell him the winner, so I guessed a horse called Clever Bill—and it came in last! That was in May, and I have never since felt that I know everything. I'm sure I lost my magic by taking the ten dollars. Magic and money don't mix."

Avis said, "You mean, Bill, that I oughtn't to tell anyone, even my mother, that I can do whatever I like? Just in case her friends try to make money out of me?"

Bill nodded. "I'm sure that's how it is."

Avis looked a little sad as she said, "Thank you, Bill. I'll have to change my plans. I'd thought of winning the hundred-dollar skating competition at the New Year Ice Carnival—I haven't ever skated, but it looks fun. And I'd thought of teaching my dog to sing real songs while I played the guitar. And I'd thought of growing a new red flower with my name written in white on its petals, which would come out only on June tenth—that's my birthday."

"Mine too," said Bill.

"And flying round and round the White House at Washington, just to amuse the President. Like this . . ."

Avis suddenly jumped into the air, glided around a big maple tree, picking a leaf from the top

15

branch as she went by, and then lay down in the air about three feet from the ground as if she were on a sofa. She said, "I'm not showing off, Bill, I promise. I'm just telling you how easy it is for me to do things."

"*Please* be careful, Avis," said Bill. "If your magic went away, you'd feel so lost and empty inside."

"But it's far more fun to do things like this if someone is watching and knows that I really can do them. I'm lucky to have *you*, Bill. I trust you."

"Oh, I wish, I wish, I wish I hadn't taken Uncle Tim's money," said Bill. "I wish I knew everything again. It would make life so much easier, especially school."

"Maybe you'll get the magic back one day," said Avis.

"I doubt it," said Bill. "Anyhow don't lose yours! Don't let your father and mother find out that you aren't just an ordinary little girl. Don't fly up to your bedroom through the window when they may be looking. Use the stairs! And I'd better keep this bit of needlework hidden. Your mother might ask questions about it."

Avis gave Bill a hug and said, "I *do* like you, Bill. You're my favorite friend of all. Thank you, thank you!"

Bill said, "By the way, Avis, did you dream of me before we met?"

"By the way, Avis, did you dream of me before we met?"

"Oh, yes, ever since I can remember. I guess that's because we have the same birthday."

She ran off, and Bill thought, "I'm glad she didn't fly home. Father Robson's in the next field and might have seen her."

Avis kept Bill's advice all that summer. They saw a lot of each other. Since she didn't really care about making money, or showing off to strangers, she might never have lost her magic but for another stupid mistake of Bill's.

It happened like this. One day he thought, "Maybe I could learn Avis's sort of *doing* magic, although I've lost my own *knowing* magic." He walked towards Robson's farm, and there he saw Robson's bull: a big, mean, black brute which was kept in a special field with stone walls and a padlocked iron gate. Bill had read about bullfights. He knew that in Spain the bullfighter goes into a ring where thousands of people sit watching all around. When the bull rushes up, the bullfighter holds out a red cape and steps aside to let the bull charge it instead of him. Then he keeps on making the bull charge his cape, time after time, all around the ring, and everyone cheers. And then . . .

"I'll try it," Bill said. He climbed the gate, walked towards the bull, and took off his brown jacket to act as a cape—but forgot that he was wearing a red shirt underneath! Bulls hate that color, and instead of charging the jacket which Bill held out, Robson's bull went straight for the shirt,

19

knocked him down, stuck a horn into his leg, and tossed him high in the air.

That would have been the end of Bill, if his dream hadn't come true. Avis suddenly appeared when he had been horned three times. Somehow she tamed the bull, laid Bill (who had fainted) across the bull's shoulders, jumped up behind, and made the bull gallop back to her home.

When they got there, she called to Colonel Deeds for help. But he was bird-watching somewhere, and Mrs. Deeds had gone shopping in the station wagon. So Avis grabbed bandages and all sorts of first-aid stuff from the family medicine

chest. Then she bandaged Bill's wounds, stopped the bleeding, and put Bill into the back of her mother's sports car.

In spite of the state police who tried to stop her at the crossroads, she drove ten miles at full speed to the nearest hospital, where the doctors took charge of Bill. She had forgotten about the bull, which ate most of the roses in the garden and made holes in the lawn with its hooves.

Avis had no chance of keeping the news quiet. The police wanted to know how she had managed to drive her mother's car so fast and well, and the doctors wanted to know who had bandaged Bill's leg in such a clever way, and Farmer Robson wanted to know how his bull had gotten over a locked gate! Reporters came from all the newspapers and asked her more questions and more questions, and she kept on saying, "I don't know . . . I don't know," because she had promised Bill to be careful, and it was true that she didn't know *how* she had done it all without learning. They took photographs of her and put her name in the papers as EIGHT-YEAR-OLD GIRL WONDER.

Soon the Governor called at the Deeds's house and asked to see Avis. Mrs. Deeds was very proud of the visit and let the Governor pester Avis with more questions until she got tired of answering "I don't know, I don't know." At last she burst into tears and said, "Oh, *please* go away, or you'll spoil everything! Can't you leave me and my magic alone?"

"Oh, so you do it by magic?" said the Governor, giving her a huge box of candy. "How very interesting! You mustn't cry! Will you come and show us some magic at my little girl's birthday party next Saturday?"

And before Avis could say "No, I won't! It's a secret," Mrs. Deeds answered for her. "Of course, Mr. Governor, my daughter will be *delighted*." This was how Avis lost her magic.

When Bill got out of the hospital, none the worse, she blamed him for having spoiled her fun. But she *had* saved his life, which was the important thing; and he would always be her favorite friend.

Besides, in some ways it was a relief to be ordinary again, like Bill.

About the Author

Robert Graves was born in Wimbledon, England, on July 24, 1895. His father was a poet, and Graves developed a love for poetry as a young man. He joined the military in 1914 and fought for the United Kingdom in World War I (1914–1918). Graves began publishing poetry while recovering from a battlefield injury in 1916. Much of his poetry described the beauty of nature and the results of war. After the war, he continued to publish his writing and began working at St. John's College in England. Later, he moved to the Spanish Mediterranean island of Majorca. There he completed one of his most famous works, the historical novel *I, Claudius*, in 1934. Graves moved to the United States after the outbreak of the Spanish Civil War (1936–1939). He moved back to Majorca after World War II (1939–1945). There he continued writing poetry, novels, and other works. In 1961 Graves returned to England to work as a professor of poetry at Oxford University. He published the short story "Two Wise Children" in 1966. The story fits the themes of his early poetry. It showcases the beauty of nature and looks at the loss of innocence. In real life World War I caused the loss of innocence, but in the story this loss happens after children misuse their magical powers. In all, Robert Graves published more than 140 books.